Larry
and the
Beanstalk

Story and photos by
Ann Gregoire

Published by Penticton Writers and Publishers

2

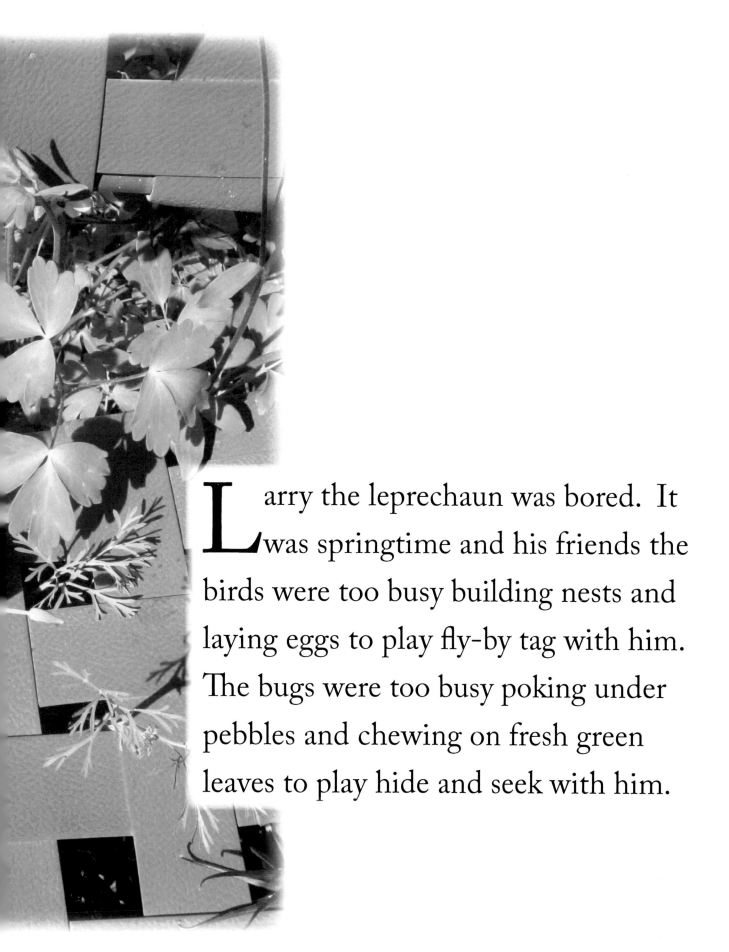

Larry the leprechaun was bored. It was springtime and his friends the birds were too busy building nests and laying eggs to play fly-by tag with him. The bugs were too busy poking under pebbles and chewing on fresh green leaves to play hide and seek with him.

"Hmmm," said Larry, "I'll have to be my own best friend today." He looked all around the secret garden searching for an adventure. The parsley wasn't tall enough to climb. The violets were annoyed when he tried to crawl under them.

Then the little leprechaun saw a gnarly branch hiding behind the clematis vine.

"Hmmm," said Larry, "that looks like a beanstalk. I remember a story about a boy named Jack who found a treasure at the top of a beanstalk; maybe I could find a treasure too!"

Larry went back to his little house under the garden bench. He might need a snack for his adventure, in case he got hungry. He looked in the cupboard, but it was empty.

"Well," said Larry, "maybe I could find something to eat on the way."

So off Larry went to climb the beanstalk, happy to start his new adventure. He climbed and climbed. He was getting tired and hungry. He stepped onto a twig, which broke off, and he nearly lost his footing! Quickly, he grabbed onto a branch to stop himself from falling to the ground below.

"Oh, goodness," said Larry. "Next time I'll wear a helmet and bring a climbing rope. This could be dangerous!"

The little leprechaun stopped and rested. "I sure wish I had some beeberries or fleerios to eat. I'm soooo hungry."

He looked way, way down. The view from so high up was beautiful. The secret garden looked so far away.

"Hmmm," said Larry. "I wonder what kind of treasure I'll find at the top of this beanstalk? Maybe a golden walnut, or a sparkly sparkler!" The thought of treasure was exciting, and Larry climbed faster.

Larry finally reached the highest branch.
He peered around, looking for the treasure.
And what did he find?

"BEANS! Ha - ha - ha! But, what else would I find at the top of a beanstalk?" He laughed so hard he nearly fell off again.

Larry was still very hungry, so he took the beans down, down, down, back to the secret garden, where he shared his treasure with his friends, the birds and the bugs.

The End

What did you find out?

1. What is Larry?

2. Where does Larry live?

3. Who are Larry's friends?

4. What does Larry hope to find at the top of the beanstalk?

5. What should Larry have brought with him to stay safe while climbing the beanstalk?

6. What is the name of another story about a boy who climbed a beanstalk to find treasure?

Raise a Reader South Okanagan extends our sincerest
appreciation to the author, Ann Gregoire, for so
generously donating *Larry and the Beanstalk.*

Library and Archives Canada Cataloguing in Publication

Gregoire, Ann, 1951-, author
    Larry and the beanstalk / story and photos by Ann Gregoire.

ISBN 978-0-9876972-4-0 (pbk.)

    I. Title.

PS8613.R44522L37 2014   jC813'.6   C2014-906254-0

Produced and distributed through
    Penticton Writers and Publshers, and
    Raise a Reader South Okanagan
with assistance from
    Yasmin John-Thorpe – Publishing Consultant
    Norma Hill – Proofreader
    Dawn Renaud – Design

Printed in Canada